For Janet, my bookselling godmother,
who gave me so many books that I love - S.T.

For Chris and Alex - K.H.

YEAHHH!

First published 2017 by Walker Books Ltd, 87 Vauxhall Walk, London SE11 5HJ • 10 9 8 7 6 5 4 3 2 1

Text © 2017 Sean Taylor • Illustrations © 2017 Kate Hindley • The right of Sean Taylor and Kate Hindley
to be identified as author and illustrator respectively of this work has been asserted by them in accordance
with the Copyright, Designs and Patents Act 1988 • This book has been typeset in Zalderdash
Printed in China • All rights reserved. No part of this book may be reproduced, transmitted
or stored in an information retrieval system in any form or by any means, graphic, written,
electronic or mechanical, including photocopying, taping and recording, without prior written
permission from the publisher. • British Library Cataloguing in Publication Data:
a catalogue record for this book is available from the British Library
ISBN 978-1-4063-6683-9 (hardback)
ISBN 978-1-4063-7434-6 (paperback)
www.walker.co.uk

THEY CAME FROM PLANET ZABALOOLOO!

SEAN TAYLOR · KATE HINDLEY

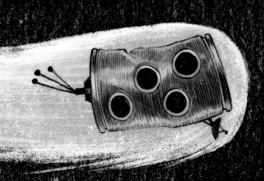

WALKER BOOKS

AND SUBSIDIARIES

LONDON · BOSTON · SYDNEY · AUCKLAND

I am Zoron. Very clever.

There is Bazoo.
He is SO
strong.

That one is Zob.
He gets overexcited and does
crazy wiggle-woggle dancing,
but we love him.

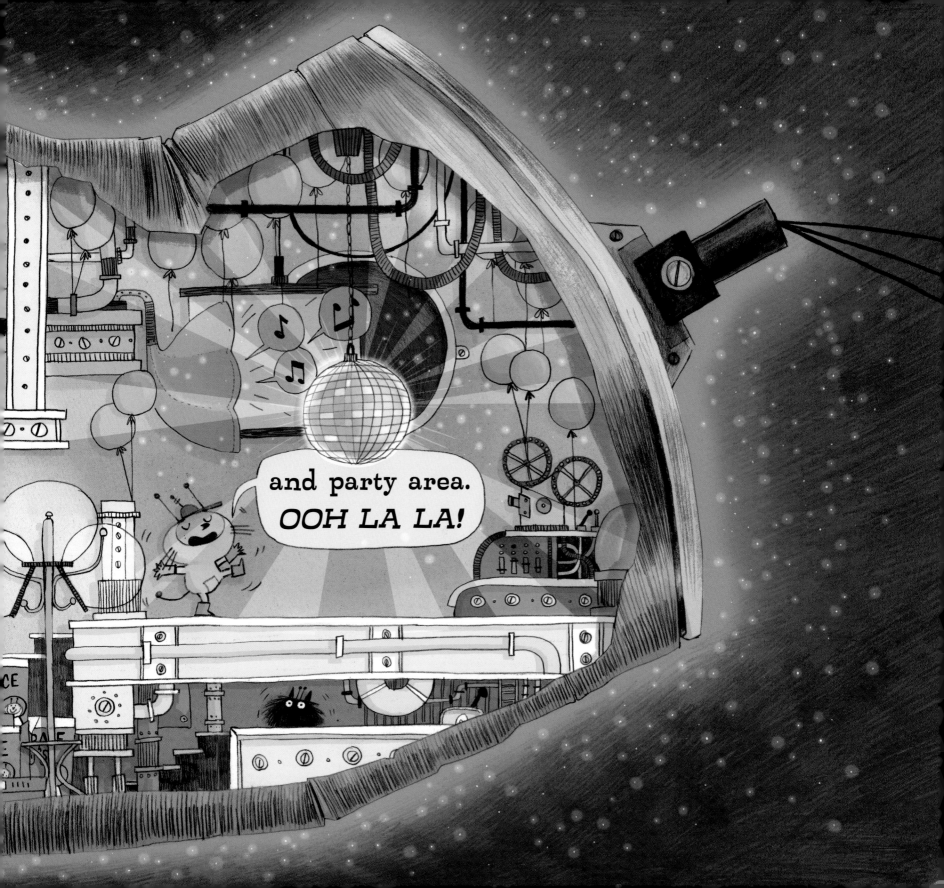

I say, "This is the chance!
Be quick and clever! Don't say
OOH LA LA or anything! OK?"

We go creeping, creeping ... like tortoise.
Bazoo has supersonic-sucker
ready!

We are going to get
BIG-SIZE thing! But Bazoo
is COMPLETE NINCOMPOOP!
He says, "I want funny photo!"
Zob says, "Okey-dokey-do!"

Then Bazoo does
silly posing for
funny photo.
We miss our chance!

Elephant makes
BIG-SIZE bottom-
trumpet sound!

The smell is too terrible!
We must go back to spaceship!

I say, "This is the chance!
Be quick and clever! No funny photo,
Zabalooloo party stuff, or anything!"

Then we go there quiet,
quiet ...

like ghosts.

Zob wants to try with supersonic-sucker!
We are going to *get* MEDIUM-SIZE thing!

But Zob is COMPLETE OVEREXCITED
NINCOMPOOP!
He does crazy
wiggle-woggle dancing!

YEAHHH!

Lion wakes up!
It wants to EAT us! Oh, boy!
We all jump up tree!

We miss
our chance!

Back in spaceship
I say,

Okey-dokey-do.
Maybe we get ...
SMALL-SIZE thing!

No one in Zabalooloo got
SMALL-SIZE thing from
planet Earth.

I say, "This is the chance! Be EXTRA quick and clever, or duck will fly away!"

Then we go there sensible like policemen.

This time *I* take supersonic-sucker.

We get closer . . .

closer . . .

closer.

But duck is SO cute. It is like cupcake!

I get overexcited!

I want funny photo!

I want to do wiggle-woggle dancing!

I am COMPLETE BIG-GOB NINCOMPOOP WITH PANTS ON INSIDE OUT!

I say,

OOH LA LA!

OH NO! NOW BEAUTIFUL SMALL-SIZED DUCK THING WILL FLY AWAY!

But no! It stays!

Zob wants to take funny photo.
I say, "OK!"
Bazoo says, "This is the chance!
Be quick and clever!
GET SMALL-SIZED DUCK
WITH SUPERSONIC-SUCKER!"

I tell him, "No! Duck is happy!
I LOVE DUCK! We leave it here!"

I give duck other biscuit.
Everyone gives it
other biscuit.

Oh, WOW-WEE!

Then I tell them, "Listen. We go home now."
Everyone says, "OKEY-DOKEY-DO!"

On the way home, we can go in party area and do Zabalooloo party stuff!

OOH LA LA!

We do crazy wiggle-woggle dancing and Bazoo gets sucked in supersonic-sucker! But he is OK.

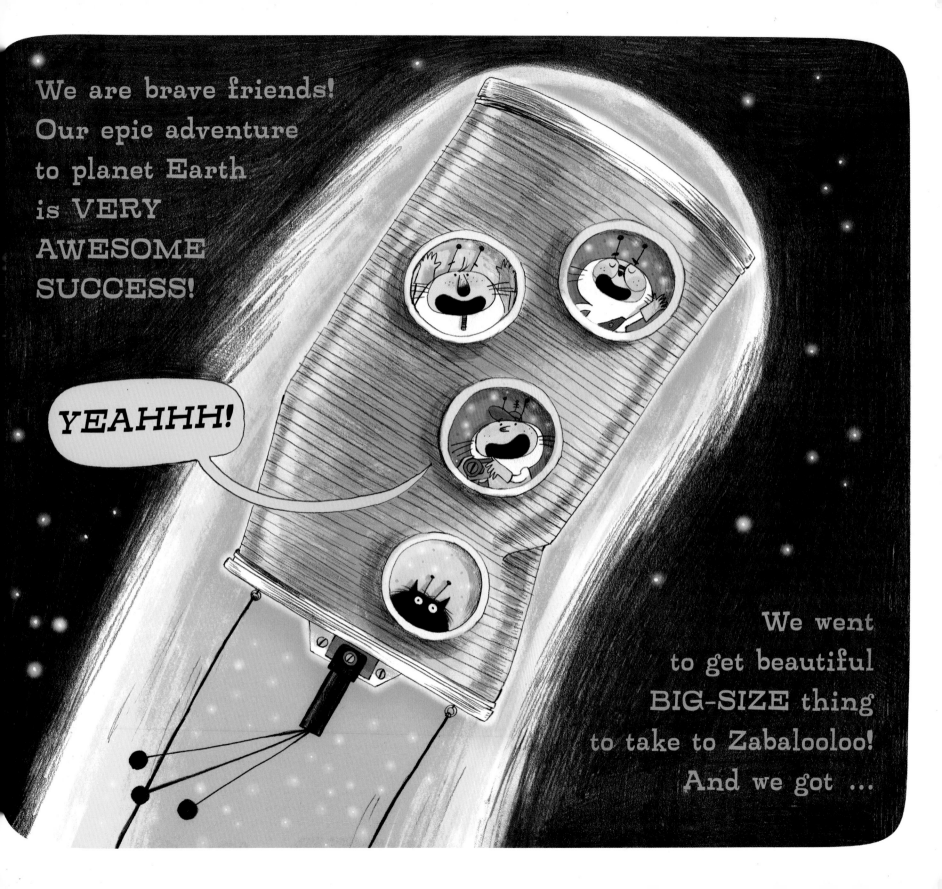